—— He has affected to render the Military independent of and
knowledged by our laws; giving his Assent to ... of pu-
nishment for any Murders which they should commit on ...
out our Consent: —— For depriving us in many cases, of the
English Laws in a neighbouring Province; establishing therein
ame absolute rule into these Colonies: —— For taking aw...
... our own Legislatures, and declaring themselves invested w...
... waging War against us. —— He has plundered our seas, ra...
rcenaries to compleat the works of death, desolation and tyranny,
... a civilized nation. —— He has constrained our fellow Citize...
...hemselves by their Hands. —— He has excited domestic insur...
...arfare, is an undistinguished destruction of all ages, sexes and co...
... been answered by repeated injury. A Prince, whose character
...ons to our British brethren. We have warned them from time to
...nigration and settlement here. We have appealed to their native
...ld inevitably interrupt our connections and correspondence
...nces our Separation, and hold them, as we hold the rest of man...
... America, in General Congress, Assembled, appealing to
...olemnly publish and declare, That these United Colonies
...d that all political connection between them and the State of G...
...conclude Peace, contract Alliances, establish Commerce, and to a...
...n, with a firm reliance on the protection of divine Providence, ...

John Hancock   Robt Morris

Larry Gets Lost in Philadelphia

Illustrated by John Skewes
Written by Michael Mullin and John Skewes

SASQUATCH BOOKS
SEATTLE

Many thanks to Lydia Bassett and Linda Calkins,
my favorite Philadelphians

Manufactured in China by C&C Offset Printing Co. Ltd. Shanghai,
China, in July 2013

Published by Sasquatch Books
17 16 15 14 13   9 8 7 6 5 4 3 2 1

Editor: Susan Roxborough
Project editor: Michelle Hope Anderson
Illustrations: John Skewes
Book design: Mint Design
Book composition: Sarah Plein

Library of Congress Cataloging-in-Publication Data is available.

ISBN-13: 978-1-57061-792-8

Sasquatch Books
1904 Third Avenue, Suite 710
Seattle, WA 98101
(206) 467-4300
www.sasquatchbooks.com
custserv@sasquatchbooks.com

This is **Larry.**   This is **Pete.**

DD-313

They like riding together
In the backseat.

Today they were headed
Somewhere brand new.
They drove their red car
Across a bridge painted **blue**.

PENN'S LANDING
This is the waterfront area where
William Penn, founder of the state of
Pennsylvania, docked in 1682.

PHILADELPHIA

THE BENJAMIN FRANKLIN BRIDGE
At 1,750 feet from tower to tower, this was the longest suspension bridge when it was completed in 1926. It connects Philadelphia, Pennsylvania, and Camden, New Jersey.

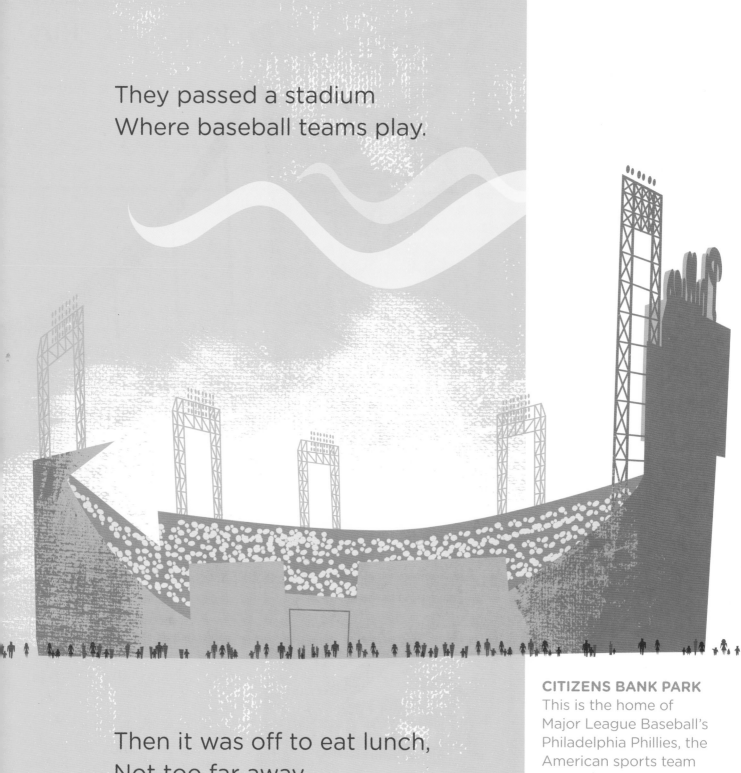

They passed a stadium
Where baseball teams play.

Then it was off to eat lunch,
Not too far away.

CITIZENS BANK PARK
This is the home of
Major League Baseball's
Philadelphia Phillies, the
American sports team
that boasts the longest
continuous time with the
same name and in the
same city (since 1883).

Dad ordered three sandwiches
(All "with Whiz"),
While poor Larry was left
To look around for his.

In a place like this,
Scraps were easily found.
When he ran to get one . . .

PAT'S AND GENO'S
Pat's King of Steaks (opened in 1930) and Geno's
Steaks (1966) stand across the street from each other.
Pat's is credited with inventing the city's signature
sandwich, the Philly cheesesteak.

Pete was no
Longer around!

There was no time to lose!
Larry had to find Pete.
He began his search
On an old-fashioned street.

ELFRETH'S ALLEY
People have lived here
continuously since 1702,
making this one of the
oldest residential streets
in the United States.

BETSY ROSS HOUSE
Built around 1740, this is believed
to be the house where Betsy Ross
lived. She is often credited with
sewing the first American flag,
but it may not be true.

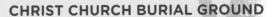

CHRIST CHURCH BURIAL GROUND
Nearly 300 years old, this cemetery
is the final resting place of Benjamin
Franklin and four other signers of the
Declaration of Independence.

Through a fence he saw a yard
With rows of carved rocks.

And a little house with a big flag
After walking two blocks.

Larry came to a house made out of thin air.
It was easy to see that Pete wasn't there.

FRANKLIN COURT

Two "ghost structures" mark the site where Ben Franklin's house once stood on Market Street. Franklin was one of the Founding Fathers of the United States. A leading author, printer, politician, postmaster, scientist, musician, and inventor, Franklin is sometimes called "the first American" because of his influence on the formation of the country.

PASS AND STOW
PHILADA
MDCCLIII

LIBERTY BELL
Forged in 1752, the bell hung in the
steeple of the Pennsylvania State
House (later called Independence
Hall) and became an iconic symbol
of American independence. It reads,
"Proclaim LIBERTY throughout all the
land unto all the inhabitants thereof."
It originally cracked soon after its
arrival from London.

Larry found a big bell
With a crack running down it.
Don't blame me, Larry thought.
I didn't do it!

INDEPENDENCE SQUARE

OLD CITY HALL

INDEPENDENCE HALL
This is where the Declaration of Independence (1776) and the Constitution of the United States (1787) were signed.

He saw a tall brick building
In a crowded city square.
Something very important
Must have happened in there.

CONGRESS HALL

GEORGE WASHINGTON
One of the Founding Fathers of
the United States, Washington was
the commander of the Continental
Army during the American
Revolution. He presided over the
creation of the Constitution and
was the country's first president.

A guy way up high seemed to
Point down the street.

He had a good view.
Could he have seen Pete?

CITY HALL
At 548 feet, this was one of the tallest
skyscrapers in the world when it was completed
in 1901. It's still the largest municipal building in the
country. It's even bigger than the United States
Capitol. Until 1987, no building in the city could
be higher than the brim of William Penn's hat!

While Pete searched a park
In the middle of the city . . .

Larry explored a fun place
That made him feel "itty-bitty"!

RITTENHOUSE SQUARE
One of the five town squares originally planned for Philadelphia by William Penn in the 1600s, the neighborhood has become one of the most famous and desirable addresses in the city.

YOUR MOVE
Daniel Martinez,
Renee Petropoulis,
Roger White, 1996

CLOTHESPIN
Claes Oldenburg,
1976

Pete worried about Larry
While surrounded by art.

BARNES FOUNDATION
Albert C. Barnes was a successful physician and
chemist whose private art collection is one of
the most valuable in the world. He arranged his
paintings in groups with furniture and other objects.

And in that moment,
Larry felt Pete in his heart.

JFK PLAZA
This plaza is know as
"LOVE Park" because
of the famous *LOVE*
sculpture by Robert
Indiana, placed there
in 1976.

Frogs, turtles, and swans
Couldn't help the lost pup.

But Larry saw a statue
That told him not to give up.

SWANN MEMORIAL FOUNTAIN
Also known as "The Fountain of the Three Rivers," the sculpted figures represent the area's three major waterways: the Delaware, the Schuylkill, and the Wissahickon.

ROCKY BALBOA
This statue depicts actor Sylvester Stallone as the boxer who famously ran up the steps of the Philadelphia Art Museum in the film *Rocky*. The statue was made for a scene in *Rocky III*.

Next up was a mountain
Of stairs to climb.
Larry braced himself,
Then took them two at a time!

PHILADELPHIA MUSEUM OF ART
Completed in 1928, it is one of the largest museums in the United States, welcoming nearly one million visitors every year.

At the top was a man who asked,
"Are you all alone?"
He checked Larry's collar,
Then took out his phone.

Pete was so happy
When that call came through.
Dad made plans to meet
Larry and the man . . .

At the zoo!

PHILADELPHIA ZOO
Opened in 1874, this is the first zoo in the United States.

The sun went down
As they drove away.

It had been an exhausting, adventurous day!